WITH LOVE TO JOHN SONCRANT

PATRICIA POLACCO
SOMETHING ABOUT HENSLEY'S

PHILOMEL BOOKS

There's just something about Hensley's! You see, no matter what a body may
need, you're sure to find it there. Why, they have everything from clothes-
pins to model airplanes. Antiques to fiddle strings. Makeup to hornet
spray to scrumptious candy counters filled with goodies.

On any given day, townsfolk gather there. They just find themselves leaning
back and talking to Old John Soncrant himself. He owns Hensley's now.
Sometimes patrons linger there, not even knowing why.

One thing is Old John is downright magical, or so folks think around here. He's the heart of that store. He has warm eyes that crinkle and dance, a sweet smile and a comforting hug for whoever may need one.

And it doesn't matter what anyone comes in to buy, Old John always has it!

Why, there was the time Therma Mosswood came in, all in a dither. "I have a catastrophe, Mr. Soncrant," she said. "My bridge club is coming today and I need one more place setting of Garden Rose dishware—by noon! It's a discontinued pattern and no one has it. I've been everywhere."

No sooner had her words hit the air than Old John was holding up two boxes of Garden Rose dishware!

"Why, that's the very thing!" Miss Mosswood said breathlessly.

And then there was the time that Tommy Ivo dashed into the store all out of breath and vexed with botheration. "Mr. Soncrant, I have a track meet in fifteen minutes and the cleats just broke off from one of my track shoes—" No sooner had Tommy said it than Old John was holding a shoe box.

"But what a shame, Tommy," he said. "There is only one track shoe in here. I don't rightly know what could have happened to the other."

Tommy took the box. "It's the left shoe, Mr. Soncrant. Exactly the one I need. And it's my size! Why, it's the very thing."

Tommy Ivo won his race that day!

And who doesn't know about the day little Sally Turnbow came into the store so worried that it took four handfuls of gumdrops to calm her down. She had broken her mother's favorite lamp and didn't know what to do. "Momma said that lamp was the only one like it in the whole world!" she wailed.

Old John went into his back room and out he came holding a very unusual lamp. "Was it something like this?" he asked.

"Why, that's it!" Sally exclaimed. "It's the very thing!"

One day, two little girls came timidly into the store. They pressed their faces up against the candy case.

"Can I help you with something?" Old John asked them.

"We're just looking," the older girl said nervously.

"We don't have any money," the younger one blurted out.

Old John smiled. He'd heard a mother'd moved into town with two little girls, alone.

"I'm Molly," the older one said. "And this is my little sister, Kate."

"How about I give you both a bag of candy to welcome you to Union City?" Old John said as he stepped behind the candy counter and shoveled delicious morsels from the bins with a metal scoop.

"I have the very thing for you. A bag of licorice for you, Molly, a bag of caramels for you, Kate, and a bag of chocolate-covered cherries for your mom." Old John smiled. "Don't be strangers now. You two and your mom, come see me anytime. You can find anything here at Hensley's, don't you know."

From that time on, Kate and Molly made Hensley's a regular stop on their way home from school. Molly perused the books for sale at the back of the store. Kate dreamed over the stuffed gingham kittens.

"I'll bet you'd like a real little kitten, wouldn't you, Kate?" Old John asked one day.

"Always," Kate said wistfully. "But Molly's allergic to them."

"Does your mother know there are shots that Molly could take so that you could have a kitty and it wouldn't bother her?" Old John asked.

"Hmm, well . . . we're renting," Kate said. "We can't have any pets."

Mr. Soncrant thought there was more to her story.

One day, a sweet, exuberant woman bounded into Hensley's. "Mr. Soncrant, I'm Mary McCafferty. Kate and Molly are my girls." She thrust her hand toward Old John. "They sure love coming to this store." Mrs. McCafferty shook Old John's hand vigorously. Then she looked at her watch. "I wonder where they are now? I was supposed to meet them here and we were going to have an early dinner at the diner." She rechecked her watch.

Just then the front door of the store crashed open and Kate came bursting in. "Momma, Molly can't breathe!" Kate cried.

Mary rushed over to the door and found Molly wheezing and gasping for air.

"Now wait," Mr. Soncrant said as he helped Molly and her mother to the back of the store. "I have a steamer. I'll set it up right away."

Mr. Miller, the village pharmacist, was in the next aisle and looked around the corner. "Does she have a rescue inhaler?" Molly's mom shook her head no. "I can run and get one right now. But I need a prescription!"

About then a round, jolly-looking man peered out from the fishing rods.
"I'm a doctor . . . perhaps I could be of assistance," he said as he took a stetho-
scope from his bag. "I'll need that inhaler, a nebulizer and a chest pack, pronto."
He drew a syringe, filled it from a small vial and gave her a shot.

"She should breathe much easier now." In no time, Molly could breathe!

Molly's mother looked at the doctor. "I . . . I can't pay you, Doctor," Mrs. McCafferty said, her eyes filled with tears.

Old John took the doctor aside.

"This little family seems to be having such a hard time, Doctor," Mr. Soncrant began. "But I can plainly see that you are a champion fisherman—I saw you admiring the antique rod and reel in the front winder."

The doctor nodded yes.

"Well, sir, I have this here old tackle box stuffed clean full of the finest fly lures there ever were." The doctor's eyes widened. "They are all hand-tied, don't you know. Each one, one of a kind."

"Are you offering those lures to me?" the doctor asked as he tried not to show how much he wanted them.

Old John nodded.

The doctor pondered for a moment. "Tell you what. You throw in that antique rod and reel, and going forward, I'll treat that child free of any charge," the doctor said.

"Done deal, Doctor!" Old John beamed.

They went over to Mary and the girls.

"I'm Doctor Case, Mrs. McCafferty; you bring your girl over to my office in Coldwater tomorrow. We'll do everything we can to get Molly's asthma under control."

Mary cried and hugged Doctor Case. Then she hugged Old John and, finally, her girls.

"I told you, Momma," Kate said, "Hensley's has everything—even a doctor to help Molly."

After that, Mary was a believer in Hensley's. She, too, became a regular. One night she stayed late just to talk to Old John. She told him the whole story, that the girls' father had left, that she was a single mom and a college student, and that her landlord had raised her rent for the second time in a year. "I just don't know what I am going to do."

Old John said, "Things will change for you, Mary. I can feel it."

One day when she stopped in, Mary noticed Old John clearing off a whole section of shelves.

"Always wanted to sell genuine hand-painted pottery. Don't you reckon the store needs something like that?" Old John asked Mary with a twinkle in his eye.

Mary looked surprised. "But . . . John, did you know I used to be a potter? I threw my own pieces, designed and painted them, too."

"Pshaw, you don't say. You, a potter?"

Mary smiled and nodded.

"Well, Mary! You're exactly what I'm looking for. You don't suppose you could make some for me? Maybe I could sell some of your pottery right here at Hensley's."

"Oh, John, it's been years. My pottery wheel is in storage. Besides, I'd need a kiln to fire the pieces and I don't even have one anymore."

Old John's eyes twinkled as he led Mary downstairs, through the antiques store and then through a back room door. In the corner of the furnace room, he pulled at a tarp, and there it was. A kiln! "I traded Old Lon Fury for it two years back. He even threw in all of these glazes." John pointed to rows and rows of colors.

"Do I dare dream," Mary whispered.

"It would be a dandy way to earn that extra money you need, wouldn't it?" Old John sang out.

Mary thought for a time. "Mr. Soncrant," Mary said dreamily, "I think we are in business."

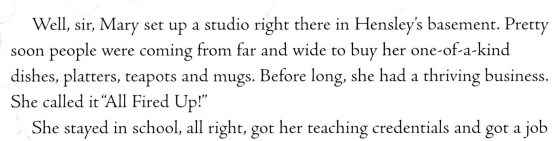

Well, sir, Mary set up a studio right there in Hensley's basement. Pretty soon people were coming from far and wide to buy her one-of-a-kind dishes, platters, teapots and mugs. Before long, she had a thriving business. She called it "All Fired Up!"

She stayed in school, all right, got her teaching credentials and got a job teaching. With that and the sale of her pottery, she and the girls were able to buy a sweet little house with a big front porch and a hanging swing.

Hensley's, of course, had the perfect paint colors, the exact wallpaper and just the right curtains for the windows. Always the very thing that was needed to make a house a home.

Molly, Kate and their mom had everything they wanted. Almost.

One day, Molly and Kate marched into Hensley's on their way home from school.

Kate had something on her mind. "Everybody in my family got just what they needed at Hensley's, Mr. Soncrant. What do I need?" Kate asked.

"Here, Kate, you need this basket, and Molly, you need this step stool," Old John said. The girls looked puzzled. "And when you leave the store, take High Street home."

"But High Street is two blocks out of our way!" Molly grumbled.

"Take it anyway, girls," he said as he whisked them both to the front door and popped chocolate raisins into each of their mouths.

"This basket is heavy!" Kate whined as she dragged it along.

"This step stool isn't exactly light, Kate!" Molly snapped.

About then, the tiniest sound seemed to be coming from directly above them.

They looked up. At first they didn't see anything, but then they heard it again. A faint little cry. The leaves rustled and moved. That's when they saw, barely clinging to a branch, a tiny, fluffy, sweet little kitten. Not two blocks from Hensley's.

"Do you suppose this is the very thing?!" Kate sang out.

Molly quickly set up the step stool, climbed up and rescued the little kitten. Kate held the basket as Molly gently dropped the kitten in, then it purred and nestled into Kate's arms as if it was meant to be there.

"Oh, Molly, Mr. Soncrant . . . he . . . why, it IS the very thing," Kate whispered as she stroked its wee little head.

"Kate," Molly whispered, "if we hadn't had this basket and the ladder, and if we hadn't come this way, we wouldn't have found this kitten." Then they looked at each other.

"Hensley's," they whispered in awe.

Well, Kate and Molly named that little cat Hensley. And, do you know, they loved that little kitty so much that from that time on, whenever they thought about their dad being gone, they were full of so much love, they didn't feel sad anymore.

They found out what everyone in Union City knows. There's something about Hensley's, and Old John, too. They also know: "There isn't anything that you can't find at Hensley's, and whatever that may be, it will always be the very thing."

POL

6 2 3 8 12 12

Patricia Lee Gauch, Editor

PHILOMEL BOOKS
A division of Penguin Young Readers Group.
Published by The Penguin Group.
Penguin Group (USA) Inc., 375 Hudson Street, New York, NY 10014, U.S.A.
Penguin Group (Canada), 90 Eglinton Avenue East, Suite 700, Toronto, Ontario, Canada M4P 2Y3 (a division of Pearson Penguin Canada Inc.).
Penguin Books Ltd, 80 Strand, London WC2R 0RL, England.
Penguin Ireland, 25 St. Stephen's Green, Dublin 2, Ireland (a division of Penguin Books Ltd.).
Penguin Group (Australia), 250 Camberwell Road, Camberwell, Victoria 3124, Australia (a division of Pearson Australia Group Pty Ltd).
Penguin Books India Pvt Ltd, 11 Community Centre, Panchsheel Park, New Delhi - 110 017, India.
Penguin Group (NZ), Cnr Airborne and Rosedale Roads, Albany, Auckland 1310, New Zealand (a division of Pearson New Zealand Ltd).
Penguin Books (South Africa) (Pty) Ltd, 24 Sturdee Avenue, Rosebank, Johannesburg 2196, South Africa.
Penguin Books Ltd, Registered Offices: 80 Strand, London WC2R 0RL, England.

Published simultaneously in Canada.   Manufactured in China by South China Printing Co. Ltd.
Design by Semadar Megged.   The illustrations are rendered in pencils and markers.
The text is set in 15-point Adobe Jenson.
Library of Congress Cataloging-in-Publication Data
Polacco, Patricia.
Something about Hensley's / Patricia Polacco.   p. cm.
Summary: Hensley's, a neighborhood general store, always seems to have what Molly, Kate, and their mother need.
[1. Stores, Retail—Fiction. 2. Single-parent families—Fiction.] I. Title.   PZ7.P75186Som 2006   [Fic]—dc22   2005032680
ISBN 0-399-24538-3
1 3 5 7 9 10 8 6 4 2
First Impression